Look for these

ROTTEN SCHOOL
books, too!

ROTTEN SCHOOL

BATTLE OF THE DUM DIDDYS

R.L. STINE

Illustrations by Trip Park

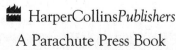

HarperCollins*Publishers*

A Parachute Press Book

For Samantha
–TP

Battle of the Dum Diddys
Copyright © 2007 by Parachute Publishing, L.L.C.
Cover copyright © 2007 by Parachute Publishing, L.L.C.

For information address HarperCollins Children's Books, a division of HarperCollins Publishers, 1350 Avenue of the Americas, New York, NY 10019.
www.harpercollinschildrens.com

Library of Congress Cataloging-in-Publication Data is available.
ISBN-10: 0-06-078833-X (trade bdg.)—ISBN-10: 0-06-078834-8 (lib. bdg.)
ISBN-13: 978-0-06-078833-9 (trade bdg.)—ISBN-13: 978-0-06-078834-6 (lib. bdg.)

Cover and interior design by mjcdesign
2 3 4 5 6 7 8 9 10
❖
First Edition

—:CONTENTS:—

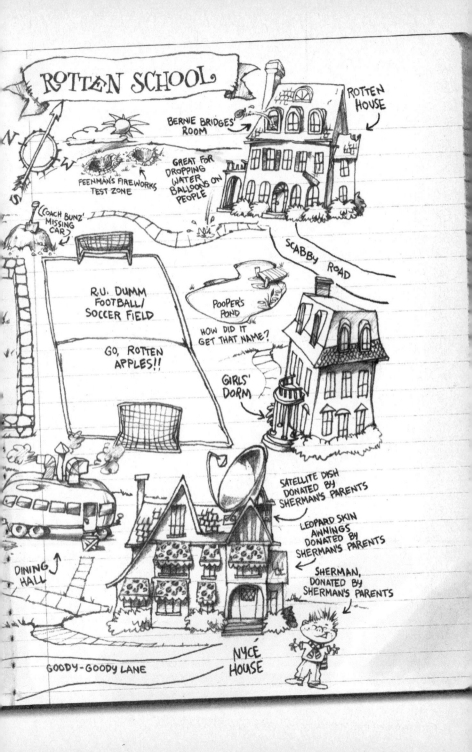

Good morning, Rotten Students. This is Head-master Upchuck, wishing you all a Rotten day. I'd like to get your morning off to a Rotten start by reading today's Morning Announcements....

First, a reminder to all students. You cannot be a member of the Membership Card Club unless you have a membership card. The only way to get a membership card is to be a member of the club.

Here's something I would like to clear up once and for all. The Official Rotten School Mascot is *not* head lice. I don't know how these rumors get started.

On the same subject, Nurse Hanley would like to remind all first graders that head lice are *not* edible. A list of proper snacks can be found in the Dining Hall.

Chef Baloney would like to thank the students who complained about the mouse in yesterday's vegetarian chili. He'd been looking all over for that mouse.

Congratulations to Mr. Boring's fifth-grade science class for your clever experiments that proved beyond a doubt that bunnies can't fly.

Chapter 1

HERE COMES TROUBLE

Was I in major trouble?

Does a moose have diarrhea in the woods?

There I was, Bernie Bridges, fourth-grade super-star. Hey, I'm not bragging. Ask anyone.

There I was, sitting with my shoulders hunched and my head down, in Headmaster Upchuck's office. And I knew the Headmaster didn't call me in to tell me a funny joke he heard.

And he didn't call me in to compliment me on the cool triple knot I tied in my blue, green, and puke-yellow Rotten School uniform necktie. (And by the way, *no way* I can untie it. I'm going to need help later—and maybe scissors—to get out of the thing!)

No, dudes and dudettes. When The Upchuck calls you to his office, it means you're in bi-i-i-i-g trouble.

Here at Rotten School, we call him The Big Man. That's because he's only about three feet tall. He's so short, he has to stand on a ladder to blow his nose!

Ha-ha. Don't you *love* jokes like that?

Well, this was no joke. I sat in front of his little toy desk. I think it came from a Barbie playhouse. It was the only desk he could find that was the right size! He was talking on the phone.

Every once in a while he'd look up at me and scowl.

I thought hard. *What did I do wrong?*

I could only think of twenty or thirty things.

Finally he set down the phone. He rubbed his ear. His bald head glowed

under the light from
his computer screen.
He turned to me.

"Bernie ..."
he said.

I didn't like
the way he
said it. I
shuddered.

*Here comes
trouble....*

Chapter 2

"I'll Bite Your Throat!"

"Bernie..." he said again.

I *still* didn't like the way he said it.

"You're looking great, sir," I said. "Are you growing taller? You look very tall today. Oh. You're sitting on a phone book, aren't you? Very clever, sir."

"Bernie—" he said.

"Mr. Upchuck, I can explain about that Go Fish game," I said. "We weren't really playing for money. I know there was a lot of money there. But we were just using it to steady the table. You see, the card table was very wobbly. And we used the money to—"

"Bernie—" he interrupted. His face turned as red as a ruby grapefruit. He actually looks a *lot* like a grapefruit. With eyes.

"Sir, I *swear* I didn't cheat on the eye exam," I said. "Someone gave me the sheet of paper with the letters on it. But I never read it. Really. I—"

He sighed. "Bernie—" he said.

"You *are* looking awesome today," I said. "Is that a shadow on your forehead? No. I think you're starting to grow eyebrows!"

"Bernie," he said through gritted teeth. "Shut your piehole."

"Yes, sir," I said, giving him a sharp, two-fingered salute. "Anything you say, sir. That's the Bernie Bridges motto. Anything the Headmaster says is gold. *Gold!*"

The Headmaster let out a sharp growl. "Say one more word, Bernie, and I'll bite your throat."

I laughed. "Funny, sir," I said. "I *love* your sense of humor. We all do. It's what makes you so special to us. You inspire us, sir. You really do. We think a new library should be built in your honor, sir. The Upchuck Library. It has a nice ring to it—doesn't it?"

"Grrrrrrrr!"

I'd never heard a sound like that from the Headmaster before.

He roared. Reached out
his pudgy hands, ready to strangle
me. And leaped over his desk.

I don't know *why* he wanted to
attack. I was being so nice to him.
But I really think The Big Man
wanted to bite my throat.

Luckily, the phone rang.

A very exciting and frightening
phone call.

But I can't tell you everything in one chapter—
can I? Keep reading....

Chapter 3

THE END OF ROTTEN SCHOOL?

Headmaster Upchuck slid back into his chair and raised the phone to his ear. "Upchuck here," he said.

His little hamster eyes narrowed to slits. "Uh-huh," he muttered as he listened. "Uh-huh."

He waved me away. "Bernie, go sit out in the hall," he said. "I'll get to you in a minute. This is an important call."

I saluted again and walked out of the office. But I didn't go sit in the hall. I hunched behind the office door. How else could I listen in on the important phone call?

I wasn't snooping. I was doing my job. The other guys count on me to know everything that's going on.

So I held my breath and pressed my ear to the door.

"I see. I see," The Upchuck kept repeating.

Peeking through the door opening, I could see a worried expression on his face. If he had eyebrows, they'd be all scrunched up.

"The Board of Inspectors is coming?" Upchuck said into the phone. "When? In one week?" He nodded his head. "Yes, I understand. Everything must be running smoothly. Yes. If Rotten School isn't up to their standards, the school will be shut down."

I gasped.

Shut down Rotten School? Impossible!

"Do you think we might have more than one week to prepare?" Upchuck asked. "Maybe a year or two?"

He sighed. "I see. Yes, I understand. One week. If the inspectors file a bad report, the school will be closed forever."

I gasped again. This was kinda serious. I mean, you probably go home after school every day. But our school is a boarding school. That means we *live* here. We can do whatever we want. No parents!

If Rotten School closed, *we'd have to move back HOME!*

"Buh-buh-Bernie—get in here!" Headmaster Upchuck called.

I was thinking so hard, I didn't even see him hang up the phone. I stepped back into his office.

He stood beside his desk. His little body trembled and shook. His lips were moving up and down, but no sound came out. I guess he was a little stressed.

"What did you want to see me about, sir?" I asked.

"Buh-buh-buh-buh." His lips kept moving up and down.

"Yes, sir?"

"Buh-buh-buh-buh-buh."

"Okay, sir," I said. "I understand." I pretended he was speaking words. I mean, the phone call had him totally shook. Why upset the poor guy even more?

He pointed a finger at me. "Buh-buh-buh-buh-buh," he said. Then his tongue flopped out of his mouth and just hung there.

"Very good, sir," I said. "Thank you for those words of wisdom. I'll never forget them."

"Lamf-lamf-lamf-lamf," he said. His tongue flopped over his chin.

"Thank you, sir," I said. I nodded solemnly. "You're totally right." I turned and hurried out of his office.

I ran across the campus, all the way back to Rotten House. That's the dorm where my buddies and I live. It's actually a rickety, old house.

I ran up the stairs to the third floor. I couldn't wait to tell my friends the big news.

Feenman and Crench were in the room they

share with Belzer, across the hall from mine. Feenman was down on his knees on the floor, painting his dresser mirror red. That's Feenman's hobby—painting things red.

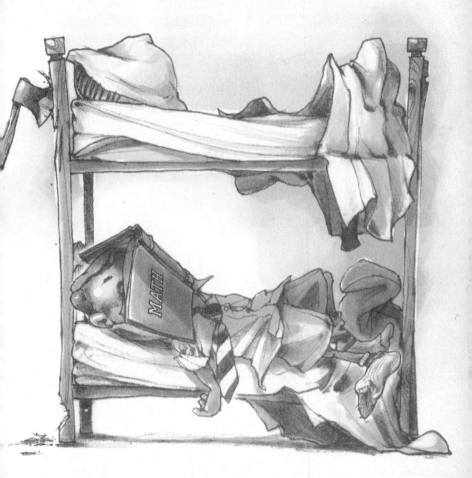

Crench was stretched out on the bottom bunk. He had a book over his face, but he wasn't reading it. He was sound asleep.

I shook him hard and woke him up. "Dudes, you

won't *believe* this!" I cried. I told them what I'd heard in Upchuck's office.

Crench shook his head. "Is it for real? The inspectors might shut this school down in one week?"

I nodded.

"They can't do that!" Feenman cried. "I just painted my dresser mirror red!"

Did that make sense? Not to me. But what do you expect from a dude who paints things red?

"Let's get serious. You know what this means—don't you?" I asked.

They stared at me.

I saw tears start to run down Feenman's cheeks. "It...it means an AWESOME school will be closed," he sobbed.

"No!" I said. "That's *not* what it means. It means we have *one week* to make as much money as we can!"

I pushed them toward the door. "Come on. Let's get moving. This could be our *last week* to cash in!"

Chapter 4

GOOD LUCK

"Okay, huddle up, dudes! Gather around!" I shouted.

The first graders were just coming out for recess. They made a circle around me. I like first graders. They're so cute—and most of them don't cry when I take their money.

"Hurry up, Bernie," a big kid with bright orange hair and freckles growled. "We only have fifteen minutes for recess."

"What do you do at recess?" I asked him.

"Kick each other," he said.

I squinted at him. "You're joking—right?"

He gave me a hard kick in the knee. I guess he *wasn't* joking. I grabbed the kid by his school blazer. "What's your name, dude?"

"Joshua," he said. "Joshua Bradly Belcher."

I decided to ignore this clown. Time to get to work.

I held up a stack of tickets. "Listen carefully, dudes!" I shouted. "Only one chance to buy these special tickets. Get your money out. Only a dollar each."

Several little angels reached into their pockets for their money. That's why I like first graders. Totally adorable.

But the big, redheaded kid raised his paw in the air. "Are they lottery tickets?" he asked. "Is there a prize?"

"No. No prize," I said. "Okay, who's first? Tell you what. I'll give you a break. Three tickets for two dollars."

The big kid was blocking the line. "But what kind of tickets are they?" he asked. "What are they good for?"

"They're Good Luck tickets,"
I said. "Everyone wants good
luck—right? Good Luck tickets
for only a dollar!"

The cute little angels waved their money in the
air. I started to drool. This was so EASY.

But Joshua Bradly Belcher poked his freckled face
up against mine. "How do we know they're *real*
Good Luck tickets?" he asked.

"Check 'em out," I said. I
held up a ticket. "It says
GOOD LUCK right on it."

The kids all stared at the
ticket. They pushed forward.
They wanted their tickets.

"Okay, one at a time. One
at a time," I said. I reached
for the first dollar. And felt
someone squeeze my
shoulder.

I looked up—and saw Mrs. Twinkler, the Drama Coach. "Come with me, Bernie," she said. She tightened her hold on my shoulder and dragged me away.

"Kids—wait right there!" I cried. "Don't anybody move."

But they'd already started kicking one another.

Mrs. Twinkler pulled me across the lawn to a shady spot under an apple tree.

"Bernie..." she said.

I hated the way she said it.

"I can explain about the Good Luck tickets," I said. "I was giving them out free. Would you like one?"

She took the ticket from me. "Bernie,

you sparkle and shine!" she said.

She talks like that all the time. She's very dramatic. She's always telling us to reach for the stars. But since the stars are about a billion miles away, I don't really get it.

"I was watching you trying to sell those tickets,"

she said. "And I was so *impressed* with you, Bernie."

Huh? Did she say *impressed*?

"You glow!" she said. "Such energy! Like a blazing star lighting up the solar system!"

"Yes, I know," I said.

"The way you hold an audience," she said, "wow, wow, wow."

"Oh, I get it," I said. "You want me to star in the school play?"

She flashed me a twinkling smile.

"I *loved* the last school play you did," I said. "What an awesome show. The kid who played Scooby Doo was terrific. I *really believed* he was Scooby Doo!"

"Thank you, Bernie," she said, still grinning at me.

"So what part do you have in mind for me?" I asked. "Of course, it's a *starring* part. Right?"

"Forget the school play," she said. "I have a better idea."

"A better idea?"

Mrs. Twinkler grabbed both of my shoulders. "I'm going to put you in charge of the annual school pageant," she said. "You'll be the pageant director."

"Really? How much does the job pay?" I asked.

"This year the pageant is something really exciting," she said. "Wow, wow, wow. It's a reenactment of the Battle of Rotten Town from 1650."

"Wow, wow, wow," I said. "I'll get busy on that right away, Mrs. T. How much does it pay?"

"This pageant is going to be WONDERFUL!" she cried. "FABULOUS! Oh, my! Did I say GLORIOUS?"

"I'll do my best," I said. "Does the director get paid?"

"I'll order the costumes," she said. "I'll have them sent to your room. And I'll get the script to you as soon as I finish it!"

She slapped me on the back. "Sparkle and shine!" she cried. "This is so exciting! Wow, wow, wow!"

"You can count on me," I said. I watched her twinkle off to the School House.

When I turned around, Feenman and Crench were standing right behind me. "What did Mrs. Twinkler want?" Crench asked.

I shrugged. "I don't know. Some kind of pageant or something. Forget about it. No time for that. Get those Good Luck tickets out. We've got to sell, sell, SELL!"

Only six days to cash in before our school is shut down. And wouldn't you know it?

Things started to get really weird....

Chapter 5

SOMETHING ROTTEN

Yes, weird. I noticed it at dinner.

That night in the Dining Hall it was Leftover Leftover Leftovers Night. That's a very special night. It means Chef Baloney serves the most popular food left over from a week ago.

My friend Beast had a huge bowl of food piled up in front of him. He was bellowing, "Kill! Kill! Kill!" and stabbing it over and over with his knife.

Beast is a little strange. He always kills his food before he eats it. You should see what he does to two fried eggs!

With a loud battle cry Beast pushed his head deep into his food bowl and started to chew.

I leaned across the table to my Rotten House buddies. "Okay, bet time," I said. "When Beast finishes his dinner, how many pieces of food will be stuck to his face?"

This wasn't a new bet. We do it about once a week. Last week Beast had a lettuce leaf stuck to his forehead and a meatball jammed in one ear. That paid off forty dollars to the lucky winner—*me*!

"Hurry, dudes," I said. "He's getting to the bottom of the bowl. Get your bets in."

The guys just sat there. No one bet.

Beast finished his meal and opened his mouth in a deafening burp—

"URRRRRRRRRP!"

that sent disgusting, wet food chunks flying across the room. Then he started biting off hunks of his bowl. "Fiber," he said, grinning happily.

"Guys, what's wrong with you?" I cried. "His face is *covered* in food! Someone could've won big-time!"

They sat staring at me dreamily, as if they were on another planet.

That was my first clue that something was rotten at Rotten School. But...what was it?

Chapter 6

WHERE DID EVERYONE GO?

After dinner I hurried over to Feenman and Crench. "Okay, dudes," I said. "This way to the Go Fish tournament. Did you tell everyone to meet behind the Student Center?"

"Not tonight, Bernie," Feenman said. "We can't."

"It's just five dollars to play," I said. "Didn't you spread the word? We only have six more days till the school shuts down."

"Sorry, Big B," Crench said. "We can't play Go Fish. You already won all our money. And we're kinda busy tonight."

Busy?

I squinted at them. "You guys are *busy* tonight? Doing what? Cleaning out your noses?"

They both laughed. "I did that at dinner," Feenman said. Then they hurried away.

As I walked back to the dorm, I didn't see a single kid.

Where *was* everyone?

The next day was just as strange.

At lunch in the Dining Hall, I stood up and made an announcement. I knew my big bulldog, Gassy, was the only dog on campus. A lot of other kids missed their dogs.

"Who wants to walk Gassy?" I asked. "Only two dollars, and you can pretend he's yours and walk him as long as you want."

No hands went up.

"I know he stinks," I said. "But he's all we've got. You can walk *in front* of him, and it doesn't smell too bad!"

No hands. No dog walkers.

I was striking out big-time.

After classes that afternoon, I carried my big bag of Nutty Nutty candy bars onto the Great Lawn. I sell them for a dollar each, and kids usually gobble them up. That's because they're Nutty Nutty Nutty-tritious.

But again, no one was around. Where had they all vanished to?

Finally I saw Beast loping across the grass. On all fours!

Beast likes to chase squirrels. He never catches them. He says he just likes to scare them to death.

"Beast, how about a salami-eating contest?" I said. "You against Joe Sweety. Everyone will want to bet on that one."

My guy always wins salami-eating contests. Because Beast is the only kid in school who can eat them *whole*! Last time, he ate ten whole salamis without even unwrapping them.

The dude is *awesome*—right?

Beast lowered his head and barfed up a disgusting glob of chewed-up grass. "Don't know why I keep eating grass," he said. "I guess for the taste."

"Beast, what about the salami-eating contest?" I asked.

"Too busy," he grunted.

I stared at him. "Too busy? Why is everyone telling me they're too busy?"

He didn't answer. He dropped back onto all fours and loped away.

I turned in a circle, gazing at the empty campus.

What's going *on* here? I wondered.

Where *is* everyone?

Chapter 7

TINKLE?

The next afternoon, I was walking across the Great Lawn, muttering to myself. "This school will be closed in four days. How am I supposed to cash in if everyone is hiding from me?"

"Bernie, who are you talking to?" someone asked.

I looked up to see Mrs. Twinkler staring at me. She was carrying a big, ugly, straw mask on a stick. The mask stared at me, too.

"Talking to myself," I muttered. "I talk to myself a lot. No one understands me better than I do."

Mrs. Twinkler nodded. "I see."

I pointed to the scowling mask. "What's that?"

"It's my nephew's head," she said, shaking it up and down.

"How did he lose it?" I asked. "Haircut too close?"

She laughed her twinkling laugh. "Hilarious. Wow, wow, wow. You're just a *riot*! My nephew *made* this head. I thought maybe you could use it in the pageant."

"The *what?*" I asked.

She laughed again. "Very funny. Where do you get that sense of humor? Don't ever lose it, Bernie. Remember, a laugh is as good as a tomato. Anytime."

"Excuse me?" I suddenly remembered I was supposed to be doing some kind of pageant.

"Have you chosen your cast members?" Mrs. Twinkler asked.

"Of course," I said. "I think you'll be pleased, Mrs. Twinkler. I have the *best* actors in school. They're acting their hearts out already, and we don't even have a script!"

The mask stared at me as if it knew I was lying.

"And how are the costumes I sent to you?" she asked.

"Way cool," I said. "Totally perfect. The kids all wanted to wear them to class. But I said they had to wait. I want everything to be a total secret. A big surprise—even to *me.*"

"Well, I'm glad you started work," Mrs. Twinkler

said. "Reach for the stars, Bernie. But keep your socks clean."

"Uh . . . right," I said. "We're all totally *psyched*, Mrs. T. We can't *wait* to do the pageant. What's it about again? I think I forgot."

The mask frowned at me. I could swear it stuck out its tongue.

"The Battle of Rotten Town," Mrs. Twinkler said. She squinted at me. "Are you sure you're working on this?"

"Of course," I said. "It's just that I forget things when I'm this excited. We're *all* so majorly excited," I said.

I saw my buddy Belzer slumping across the grass. Belzer is probably the most uncool dude at Rotten School. But he's a good kid. For one thing, he brings me breakfast in bed every morning. Then he carries my books to class.

He's not really a slave. He just likes to do everything I ask.

I grabbed Belzer by the shoulders and heaved his pudgy body up to Mrs. Twinkler. "Here's one of our soldiers," I said. I clapped him hard on the back.

A little *too* hard. He fell to his knees.

"Excellent fall, Belzer," I said. I turned to Mrs. T. "See how he's practicing? The dude is a real actor. He's gonna be terrific."

Belzer blinked five or six times. He always blinks when he's thinking hard. "Practicing? Practicing *what*, Bernie?"

I slapped my hand over his mouth.

"Did you ever hear such enthusiasm?" I asked her. "He's gonna steal the show!"

"Show?" Belzer mumbled behind my hand. "Is there gonna be a show? Will they have popcorn?"

"Ha-ha." I tossed back my head and laughed. "What a joker! You're gonna be proud of him, Mrs. T.!"

She flashed us her sparkling grin. "I'm proud of *both* of you," she said. "Twinkle and shine, boys. Remember—always twinkle and shine!"

She walked off, shaking her nephew's head.

"Did she say *tinkle?*" Belzer asked, blinking hard.

I pulled Belzer up from his knees. "I don't think so," I said. I brushed Belzer off.

"What kind of show was she talking about?" he asked.

"Some kind of dumb pageant," I said. "Don't worry about it. It'll never happen. The school will probably be shut down by then."

I had more important things to think about. I hurried to see my buddies, Feenman and Crench. The clock was ticking. I needed their help.

Chapter 8

GOOD MEMORIES

I ran up the two flights of stairs to my room. Their room is across the hall from mine. I could hear loud shouts and screams coming from inside.

Probably doing their Three Stooges act, I decided. Feenman and Crench love to kick and slap and head-butt each other and poke each other's eyes out. It's a total riot—especially if you like pain.

I pushed open the door and stepped inside their room. A blast of hot, steamy air hit my face. It's always hot in their room. The room used to be a closet.

"Whoa! I don't believe this!" I cried.

Feenman and Crench weren't poking and slapping each other. They were hunched over a laptop, staring at the screen. Crench frantically moved the mouse, clicking it again and again.

The shouts and cries came from the laptop.

"Give me a break," I said, stepping up beside them. "What's up with this?"

Feenman raised a finger to his lips. "Shhhh. It's the Battle of Heartburnia."

I gasped. "The WHAT??"

He shushed me again.

An armored knight on the screen had a long spear shoved through his chest. It went all the way through him and came out the other side.

"YOOOOWWWWWW!"

Feenman screamed, as if *he* was the one who got skewered.

"Bet that hurts," I muttered.

Feenman held his chest, gasping for air.

"Want a Band-Aid?" I asked.

"Shhhh." It was Crench's turn to shush me. He had his face right up against the screen. He clicked the mouse furiously. "Gotcha! Gotcha! Gotcha!" he screamed.

"We have to use our swords," Feenman told me. "We don't have enough weapon points to buy fireballs."

"We spent all our bubus on a horse," Crench said.

CLICK~CLICK~CLICK~CLICK.

"You WHAT?" I cried. "Spent all your bubus? What's a bubu? Have you both gone nuts?"

CLICK~CLICKCLICKCLICK!

"Will you two *stop*?" I screamed.

They both spun around. But Crench kept clicking the mouse. I guess he couldn't stop his finger.

"We can't take a break in the middle of a battle," Crench said. "Do you want our knights to lose the big wing-wang?"

"Stop talking baby talk!" I shouted. "You're starting

to scare me. I need you guys for a *real-life* emergency."

Feenman scratched his head. "Real life?"

"We can't help you," Crench said. "We're too busy. We're the Doo-Wah-Diddy Dragons."

Feenman nodded. His hair fell over his face. He looked a lot better that way.

"The Doo-Wah-Diddy Dragons are battling the Knighty Knight Knights," he said.

I pinched their cheeks. "You two are definitely Dum Diddys," I said. "How can you waste your time on a stupid game?"

"Wungo Warriors isn't a game," Crench said. "It's a battle to the death. If the Knighty Knight Knights win this Battle of Heartburnia, we'll have to pay a battle tax to the great Wungo Wango."

I slapped my forehead. "Please—speak English! What's wrong with you two?"

CLICK~CLICK~CLICKCLICK.

"Listen to me, dudes," I said. "Remember what I overheard in Upchuck's office? The inspectors are coming on Saturday, and they're going to shut down the school. We've got to act fast. Don't you want to go to your next school with your pockets full of bubus?"

CLICK~CLICK~CLICK.

Okay. That didn't work. I decided to try a different approach.

"Don't you care about your school?" I asked. "Don't you have any *feeling* at all for this wonderful place? Don't you have any *heart?*"

They both turned away from the laptop and stared at me.

I put my arms around their shoulders. "We're good buddies, right?" I said. "And we've had wonderful times here. Great, great memories." I let a few tears fall from my eyes.

"You okay, Bernie?" Feenman asked.

"I ... I just can't believe our school could be gone in a few days," I said. I let my voice tremble. "Don't you guys remember all the good times? Remember when Headmaster Upchuck fell into Pooper's Pond, and we had to pull a minnow out of his nose? Remember when Mrs. Heinie lost her glasses and walked right into a bulldozer? Remember when the chef accidentally put poison ivy into the salad?"

"Good times," Crench said.

"Yeah. Lotsa good memories," Feenman said.

"Well, don't you want to cash in before the good memories are gone forever?" I asked.

CLICK~CLICK~ CLICKCLICKCLICK!

Chapter 9

THE SLAUGHTER BEGINS

Belzer came bobbing into the room. He flashed me his lopsided grin. I keep meaning to take my pliers and straighten his teeth for him. That's how much I care about my guys.

"Belzer," I said, putting my arm around his shoulders. "These two guys have gone totally nutso. I'm glad to see you."

Belzer blinked several times. "What was that about tinkling?" he asked.

"Forget about that," I said. "Belzer, I've got two cases of Foamy Root Beer hidden under my bed. Pull them out and carry them downstairs. We'll sell them to the second graders for three dollars a can."

Belzer shook his head. "I can't, Big B."

Huh? Belzer saying *no*?

"Why not?" I asked.

"I'm not Belzer," he said. "I'm Prince Barfo of Barfolonia."

Has EVERYONE gone NUTS???

I hurried back to my room. "YOWWWWW!" I tripped over the big trunk on the floor—and fell on my face.

I forgot about the trunk. The pageant costumes from Mrs. Twinkler were inside.

With a groan, I pulled myself to my feet. I had to find some dudes who wanted to lose money to Bernie B. I stuffed a deck of cards into my back pocket and hurried downstairs to search the dorm.

"Don't give up, Bernie," I told myself. "You're the great Bernie B. You *can't* give up!"

You know the Bernie Bridges motto: *A quitter never wins, and a winner never gives back the bubus he's won.*

My first stop was my buddy Chipmunk's room. Chipmunk is a good guy, but he's a little shy. His hobby is hiding under the bed and pretending he's invisible.

I knocked on Chipmunk's door. He's too shy to say "Come in." So I barged right into the room.

He was hunched over his laptop.

"Yo, Chipper," I said. "How's the Chip-Chip-Chipper?"

I stepped up beside him and put a hand on his shoulder. "I'm starting a new Go Fish tournament,"

I said. "Only five dollars to play. What do you say, Chipper?"

He grabbed my hand and shoved it away. "I'm not Chipmunk," he said in a weird, deep voice. "I'm Merlo the Merciless!"

"Huh? *You*? *You're* merciless?" I cried. "Whoa, Chipmunk—"

"Merlo the Merciless spares no one!" he screamed. "I eat slabs of raw beef for breakfast! And I pick my teeth with human bones!"

I stared at him. This wasn't exactly the Chipmunk I knew. Was he *possessed*?

I lowered my eyes to his laptop screen. I saw a bunch of hooded dwarf creatures with green faces.

"The slaughter begins!" Chipmunk bellowed.

He *was* possessed. Everyone in the dorm was going berserko!

Shaking my head, I hurried back into the hall. Billy the Brain's room was next door. Billy is the biggest brainiac in school.

He's so smart, he can read his watch upside down!

The door was open. The lights were out. I poked my head in. "Billy? Are you here?"

Chapter 10

BATTLE OF THE BRAINS

Billy is so smart, he can read a book and chew gum at the same time.

"Billy? What's up, dude?" I called.

I saw him sitting between *two* computers. I slapped knuckles with him, and we did the secret Rotten House handshake.

"What's up with *two* computers?" I asked. "Does it help you do your homework twice as fast?"

"No way," Billy said. He slapped his chest. "I'm Sir Fleabagge!" he shouted. "Knightly Knight of the Knighty Knight Knights."

"Huh??"

He slapped his chest again. "And I'm battling *myself*," he boomed. "As Grand Master Mister Buff Diddy of the Doo-Wah-Diddy Doodly Diddly Dibbly Dribbles!"

I swallowed hard. "But, Billy—why are you fighting *yourself?*" I asked.

He tapped his forehead. "Don't you get it? I *can't lose!* Even if I *kill* myself, I'm still a winner!"

I *told* you the dude is a genius.

Billy clicked his mouse a few times. Then he turned to me and started to sing:

"We're the Knighty Knight Knights,
and we have no fright.
We even go outside late at night!"

He clicked some more, staring at both screens. He shouted and whooped for joy. Then he groaned a few times. A few more clicks, and he turned back to me and started to sing a different song:

"We're the Doo-Wah-Diddy Dibbly
    Dribbles,
Doo-Wah, Doo-Wah.
We're mean, we're fierce,
Our own ears we pierce,
Doo-Wah, Doo-Wah.
We curse, we spit,
We always stand, we never sit.
We can't end this song. It goes on
    too long,
But we don't know what rhymes
    with Dribbles!"

"Very catchy," I said.

CLICK~CLICK~CLICK.

"I like both battle songs," Billy said. Then his eyes bulged as he stared at the screens. "Look out!" he shouted. "I'm in a battle to the *death* with myself now!"

CLICKCLICKCLICKCLICK!

"Gotcha! Gotcha! Gotcha!"

"Ow! Ow! Owwwwww!"

I crept out and closed his door behind me. "I've gotta lie down," I said. "I'm the only dude in the dorm who isn't NUTS!"

Chapter 11

ANGEL WANTS TO KILL!

I never quit. You know my motto: *Today is the first day of the rest of your life, so cash in while you can, even if your school is going to close and every kid you know has lost his mind.*

The deck of cards was burning a hole in my pocket. But finding someone to play cards with me was tough.

Here's how desperate I was. I tried Angel Goodeboy.

He's the sweetest, most adorable, most angelic dude in school. He has pictures of angels with shiny halos on the walls in his room. The girls are all crazy about his dimpled cheeks and his blue eyes and his wavy, blond hair.

He's so totally sweet, he makes you want to hurl your lunch. But even angels like to play cards once in a while—don't they?

I knew I was in trouble when I stepped into his room and saw him at his laptop.

"I'm not Angel Goodeboy," he boomed. "I'm the Death-Face Dungeon Master."

"Cute," I said.

Angel's eyes rolled around wildly in his head. He jumped up from his chair and began waving a fist in the air.

"Know what I like to do in my dungeon?" he shouted.

"CATCH! TRAP! DESTROY! WIN!"

What an angel!

"Guess you wouldn't be interested in a little card game?" I said.

"CATCH! TRAP! WIN!"

he screamed. He let out a roar and ripped the screen off his laptop.

"Nice talking to you. Catch you later," I said.

Out on the Great Lawn, I saw Jennifer Ecch rumbling toward me. Jennifer is big and strong and husky and big and strong and husky. Get the picture? I call her Nightmare Girl because she's crazy in love with me.

How would *you* like to be in fourth grade and have a big and strong and husky girl plant smoochy kisses all over you and call you Buttercakes and

Honeyface? You'd hate it, right?

So, when I saw The Ecch walking toward me, I spun around and started to run. But, whoa. I stopped. I was desperate, remember?

I took a deep breath, turned, and walked right up to her. "Hi, Jen," I said. "Would you like to play cards with your old Buttercakes Honeyface?"

I waited for her to say yes and then grab me tightly and plant loud, smoochy kisses all over my face. But she didn't do that.

"I'm not Jen!" she boomed, raising both fists in the air. "I'm the Doo-Wah-Diddy Dum Dum Diddy Princess!"

I slapped my forehead. "Not you, too!" I cried. "Okay. Would the *princess* like to play a few rounds of poker?"

"How DARE you!" she screamed. "I'm a Third Level Dum Diddy Dribble!" Then, before I could duck away, she grabbed me around the waist. She heaved me high over her shoulders—and slammed me down to the grass.

"*Nighty-night to all Knighty Knight Knights!*" she screamed. Then she took off, galloping away, kicking up big clods of dirt as she ran.

Flat on the ground, I checked myself over. Only three or four broken bones. I should be okay. I pulled myself to my feet and limped away.

Chapter 12

THE WUNGO WANGO

Was I desperate?

Does a bear eat baby birds for dessert?

Only two more days of school, and I wasn't making a dime. And everyone in school was acting crazy and talking some weird language.

I was so desperate, I walked over to the boys' dorm we all hate and despise—Nyce House. Maybe the guys were acting normal there.

As I stepped up the front steps, my legs started to wobble, my tongue fell out over my chin, and my head started to shake, rattle, and roll.

I told you—we Rotten House dudes *hate* Nyce House. Would YOU like to live in a place called NYCE House?

Of course not.

I rolled my tongue back into my mouth. Then I opened the front door and walked into the entry hall.

It was clean and neat and bright. Lovely paintings of forests and ocean waves were on the walls. Soft music played. Guys were sitting on leather chairs and couches, reading textbooks silently.

Disgusting, right?

Coming toward me I saw my archenemy—that spoiled rich kid Sherman Oaks. Sherman is so rich, he pays a kid to take a shower for him every morning.

He flashed his perfect smile at me. His blond hair glowed under the bright dorm lights. His dark eyes popped out like two raisins in a bowl of Frosted Flakes.

"Yo, Bernie," he said. "I know why you're here."

I stared at the jagged chunk of decayed wood dangling from a chain around his neck. "Sherman, what's that? One of your baby teeth?"

He chuckled. He held up the wood chunk.

"It's a piece of the *Titanic*," he said. "You know.

That big ship that sank? Divers brought it up from the ocean bottom. This little hunk of it cost ten thousand dollars. My parents send me expensive presents to show me how much they care."

"Nice," I said.

"I know why you're here," he said again. "You've come to see the Wungo Wango."

I blinked a few times. "Sherman, who or *what* is the Wungo Wango?" I asked.

He tapped the front of his silk shirt. "*I'm* the Wungo Wango," he said.

"And I'm Batman," I said. "Sherman, go lie down. You must be running a high fever. I'll get Nurse Hanley."

"Stop joking, Bernie," he said. "You know I'm the Wungo Wango. You came here for a Wungo Bungo card—right?"

"Well...I came here to get up a card game," I said.

He stuck out his hand. "The Wungo Bungo card costs five dollars. You can pay the Wungo Wango."

If I chewed gum, I would have swallowed it.

"*I'm* going to pay *you* five dollars?" I cried.

He nodded. "Five dollars. Pay up. Everyone else

in school already has a card. When you have your card, you get your access number. It lets you enter the Kingdom of Wungo Bungo."

I slapped my own face. Was I dreaming this?

I slapped Sherman's face. He was real. I was awake. It all suddenly became clear to me.

"Is that what all the kids in school are talking about? Did they all pay you five dollars to play this game?" I asked.

"You'll enter as a Dum Diddy Drone," he said. "If you are skillful, you can work your way up to Dum Diddy Dum Dum Diddy Plebe."

Me? A *plebe*?

"Uh...couldn't I be a Wungo Wango, too?" I asked.

Sherman tossed back his head and laughed for two or three minutes. I could see the gold fillings in his teeth. His initials were carved into each one.

"Bernie, since you're so totally pitiful, I'll give you a free tour," he said.

"You're going to take me to the kingdom?" I shook my head in disbelief.

He nodded solemnly. "Follow the Wungo Wango," he said.

Chapter 13

DEATH OF
A KNIGHT

Sherman led me to his room. He had a zebra skin bedspread. The bed was bigger than my *room*. I spotted a bubbling Jacuzzi next to a small lap pool.

A poster of a huge dollar bill hung on one wall. Another poster on his closet door was a giant photo of Donald Trump. Sherman's desk glowed so brightly, I had to shield my eyes.

"It's solid gold," he said. "I just love the way gold feels—don't you?"

I started across the room.

"Bernie, take off your shoes," he said. "The

floorboards are a rare ebony from Madagascar, taken from the tusks of an extinct root hog."

I shook my head. "Sherman, why do you have all this stuff?"

He shrugged. "I want it to feel like home."

We sat down in front of his computer. He had a flat-screen monitor the size of an SUV. He leaned over the keyboard and started to type in a bunch of numbers.

"That's my access code," he explained. The bright colors on the huge monitor made Sherman's face glow blue and yellow. His eyes flashed with excitement.

"Here we are in Wungo Bungo," he said. "It's nighttime in the kingdom. See the two moons in the sky?"

I squinted at the screen. "Yeah. Two moons," I said. "Cool."

What was the big deal?

"The force of the two warring moons has divided the kingdom," Sherman said. "The war has lasted three milagoniums."

"Is that long?" I asked.

He nodded. He slid his mouse around. The colors rolled across his face. A low wooden building came into view. I could see black horses inside. I could hear them neighing softly.

"This is the stable of Wuu-Wuu," Sherman said.

"Wow, wow," I whispered.

He slid the mouse, and we moved closer to the stable. "The Knighty Knight Knights keep their horses here."

I pointed. "Who's that guy with the bucket?"

"He's Pippy the Pitiful. He's a Knighty Not Knight. He doesn't have enough weapon points to be a knight. That's why he's watering the horses."

"How does he get weapon points?" I asked.

"First he has to earn costume points," Sherman said. He moved the mouse. "See? He has chest armor, but he isn't wearing any pants."

We moved closer. Sherman was right. I could see the dude's naked butt.

"First costume points, then weapon points, then power points," Sherman explained. "He gets paid two bubus for watering the horses. In two weeks, he'll have enough bubus to buy pants."

"Hope he doesn't catch cold," I said.

Sherman gasped. "I saw something move at the side of the stable," he said. "The Dum Diddys may be planning a sneak attack."

He began sliding the mouse around frantically, clicking on bushes and trees. "Here is my best knight," he said. "Sir Sherman."

I stared at the powerful-looking knight in shining armor who stepped onto the screen. "You named him after *you*?"

"He IS me!" Sherman said. "Now, watch. I'm going to move him so he can scout around for Dum Diddys."

"Let me try it," I said. I grabbed the mouse from Sherman. "You left-click like this, right? And hold it down?" I started to move Sir Sherman toward the woods.

"Careful!" Sherman cried. "Sir Sherman is my best knight. Watch out! Don't let anything happen to him!"

"No problem," I said. I slid the mouse and moved the knight in front of the stable. "I'm so new at this," I said. "This is fun! Am I doing it right, Sherman?"

I pretended I didn't know how to slide the mouse.

"Careful!" Sherman cried. "Let me do it, Bernie. Sir Sherman is too valuable to risk."

I moved the big knight toward the stone well in front of the stable.

"Look out!" Sherman cried. "Careful! Careful! Move him away from the well!"

He tried to grab the mouse. But I held on tightly.

And I dropped Sir Sherman into the well.

I heard a loud splash. Water crashed up over the sides of the well. Then silence.

"Uh-oh," I said, pressing my hands to my cheeks. "Did I do something bad?"

Sherman's mouth dropped open as he stared at the well. "Sir Sh-Sherman?" he stammered. "My best knight? You *d-d-drowned* him!"

"I'm just not good at this kind of game," I said. "Guess I'd better stick to cards."

"Sir Sherman?" Sherman muttered, staring at the well on the giant screen. "Sir Sherman? Gone forever?" He began pounding his head on the gold desk.

THWACK! THWACK! THWACK!

Probably a good time to leave.

I climbed to my feet. "Thanks for the test run," I said.

THWACK!
THWACK! THWACK!

He just kept smacking his head on the desk.

"Looks like a whole bunch of fun," I said. "Bye!"

Chapter 14

MRS. TWINKLER IS WORRIED

At lunch the next day, I had no appetite. I could barely eat my three cheeseburgers, two plates of mac and cheese, four pizza slices, and a few pretzels.

I sat with all my buddies at the Rotten House table in a corner. At the other end of the table, Beast was making everyone sick by sucking down a long, purple worm he found on the floor. He made gross, slurping noises before he started to chew it.

I closed my eyes. I had to shut out the world and THINK.

Sherman collected five dollars from every kid in

school. They were all *desperate* to play the Dum Diddy game. What could I do to cash in, too?

After a minute or two my brain was sizzling. Smoke poured out of my ears.

Think.... *Think*....

Just when an idea started to form, someone tapped me on the shoulder.

I opened my eyes. I blinked a few times. "Oh, hi, Mrs. Twinkler," I said. "You're looking good. I love that green ribbon in your hair."

"It's not a ribbon," she said. "Some kid spit lettuce at me."

She held on to my shoulder. "Bernie, we need to have a serious talk."

Uh-oh.

Chapter 15

"SO REAL! SO FRESH!"

"Bernie, I'm worried about the pageant," Mrs. Twinkler said.

I blinked. "Pageant?"

Beast let out a roaring burp. It lasted at least a minute and made a large brown stain on the table-top.

"Don't pay any attention to him," I told Mrs. T. "He usually eats on the floor, but someone stole his food dish."

"Bernie, I hope you're not letting me down. The pageant is going to thrill our students and teachers.

It'll get raves. Raves! You'll be shining stars! But . . . have you been rehearsing?" she asked.

Rehearsing?

"Of course," I said. "We rehearse day and night, Mrs. Twinkler."

"Then how come I haven't been invited to any rehearsals?"

Think fast, Bernie. . . .

"We want it to be perfect before you see it," I said. "We're working so hard. We're desperate to make you proud of us."

"Do the costumes fit?" she asked.

"Perfectly," I said.

I wasn't lying. They fit the trunk perfectly. Too bad I'd never opened the trunk. . . .

"And what about the sets?" Mrs. T. asked. "Who is building the sets?"

Think fast again, Bernie. . . .

"Uh . . . we're not using sets," I said. "We're . . . uh . . . going to do the pageant outdoors. You know. Out on the grass. To make the battle more real."

She smiled. "Nice idea! That's *fresh*!" she said. She clapped me hard on the back. "Fresh! Very fresh! I can see you put a *lot* of thought into this."

"Oh, yes. A lot," I said.

Down the table, Beast lapped up a bowl of split-pea soup, then made it come out his nose. When Crench turned to laugh at Beast, Feenman swiped all the French fries off Crench's plate. He stuffed them into his pants pocket to eat later.

Mrs. T. pulled another lettuce leaf from her hair. "Are you really rehearsing?" she asked.

"We're rehearsing right now," I said. "See? We're not really eating lunch. We're practicing the big dinner scene. That's where the battle started in 1650."

She rubbed her forehead. "I . . . I don't remember that."

"Yes," I said, "this is the opening scene. Watch how the battle starts."

Crench turned to Feenman. "Hey—you jerk! You stole my French fries!"

"Prove it," Feenman replied.

Crench shoved his hand into Feenman's pocket and pulled out some fries. "You're a total jerk!" he shouted.

I grinned at Mrs. Twinkler. "I wrote that line," I said. "It works—right?"

Crench grabbed Feenman, and they started wrestling on the table, grunting and growling, punching each other, rolling over everyone's lunch.

"That's how the Battle of Rotten Town started," I told Mrs. T. "I did some more research."

She clapped her hands together. "So real! They look like they're really fighting!"

"Practice," I said. "Practice and hard work."

"So fresh!" she exclaimed. "Fresh and delightful!"

Feenman tugged a fistful of French fries from his pocket and shoved them into his mouth. He and Crench rolled onto the floor with a *thud* and kept fighting.

"Wonderful work!" Mrs. T. exclaimed. "Good acting. But are you sure that's how the Battle of Rotten Town started?"

"Yes, I Googled it," I said. "It started over a pants pocket stuffed with French fries."

She clapped me on the back again. "Keep up the good work, Bernie," she said. "Sparkle and shine! Sparkle and shine!"

80

I watched her hurry away.

"What was *that* about?" Billy the Brain asked.

"No big deal," I said. "Forget about it. Some play or something that's never gonna happen."

Billy nodded. He finished his last fish stick. He always has fish for lunch. He says it's brain food. He jumped up onto the table and started to sing:

"We're the Knighty Knight Knights, and we have no fright.
We even go outside late at night!
We're not afraid of anything.
We'll even climb up on a table and sing!"

To my horror, all of my buddies jumped up onto the table to sing along with him. Except for Feenman and Crench. They were still rolling around on the floor, wrestling over the French fries.

And that's what gave me my awesome idea. The idea that changed everything for Bernie B....

Chapter 16

No More Bubus

The next afternoon in my room, I listened to Feenman, Crench, and Belzer across the hall. Of course, they were playing Wungo Warriors. What else?

I could hear horses galloping and knights and monsters screaming from their laptop speakers. Feenman and Crench were screaming, too.

"You idiot!" Feenman shouted. "How could you do that?"

"It was an accident!" Crench replied.

"Now we're gonna lose the battle," Belzer moaned.

"How *could* you?" Feenman cried. "How could you spend all our bubus on *shaving cream?*"

"I thought it was armor and battle-axes!" Crench said. "I didn't know it was shaving cream!"

"We're broke," Feenman wailed. "And we have twenty barrels of shaving cream. You total moron!"

I heard the thud of bodies. Grunts and groans. I hurried across the hall to see Feenman and Crench wrestling on the floor again.

Shaking his head, Belzer turned to me. "Bernie, aren't you gonna break up the fight before they kill each other?"

GRUNT! GRUNT!
GROAN! GROAN!
THUD! THUD! THUD!

Feenman was banging Crench's head against the floor. "Shaving cream!" he screamed. "All our bubus on shaving cream!"

"*No way* I'm going to break this up," I said. "I'm gonna help them fight."

I hurried back to my room to set my plan into motion.

Chapter 17

PRINCE AWESOME DUDE ARRIVES

I dropped onto my knees in front of the big, wooden trunk. I popped the latches and pushed the lid up.

"Yes! Yes!" I cried happily.

Costumes for Mrs. Twinkler's pageant. There would never be a pageant. But the costumes wouldn't go to waste!

THUD! THUD! GROAN! GROAN! GRUNT!

I could hear Feenman and Crench wrestling across the hall.

I pulled an armor helmet over my head. I grabbed a shield and a sword from the trunk—and went running back to their room.

They both stopped fighting and stared up at me from the floor. "Bernie, what's up with the armor and the sword?" Feenman asked.

"I'm not Bernie!" I shouted through the mask. "I'm Prince Awesome Dude of the Doo-Wah Dum Dum Diddys!" I waved the sword.

Their eyes bulged. "Cool," Belzer muttered. "Is that a real sword?"

"Close enough," I said. "Dudes, why play the game on that tiny laptop screen when you can play it in *real life?*"

"Awesome!" Feenman said.

"Sweet!" Crench agreed.

I dragged the three of them into my room. I started pulling costumes out of the trunk. "Feenman, take the blue cape. It goes with your eyes. Belzer, careful with that dagger. You know you're not good with pointy things!"

They pulled iron masks over their heads. "Doo-Wah-Diddys rule!" Crench shouted.

"Only five dollars a costume," I said. "Come on, dudes. Cash only. Pay up. Pay up. And NO bubus. I only take American dollars!"

They each forked over the five bucks. I looked up to see more guys in my doorway. "Nosebleed, Chipmunk—get in here!" I pulled out more costumes.

"Five dollars. Pay up. Gimme five!" I shouted, handing out the armor and swords. "Now you dudes can play Wungo Warriors in 3-D!"

Their happy cries rang out:

"Sweet!"

"Awesomely awesome!"

"Totally gnarly!"

"Nighty-night to all Knighty Knight Knights!"

"Owwwww! You poked my eye out!"

"Beast, get in here!" I shouted. "Hey—who else is left? Don't shove—I've got plenty of costumes! One size fits all! Hurry. Get your money out."

I had a big wad of cash in my hand. The line of Rotten House guys waiting for costumes stretched down the stairs. Even Angel Goodeboy forked over five bucks for a cape and wooden sword.

After a few minutes the Doo-Wah-Diddys all stood there in their armor, holding their plastic shields, waving their swords, singing the Doo-Wah-Diddy Dragons anthem.

Belzer had his visor on sideways. He kept walking into walls. I grabbed the visor and spun it around. I heard Belzer's neck crack. Maybe I spun it too hard!

"Now what do we do, Big B?" Belzer asked.

"ATTACK! DESTROY! WIN!" Angel shouted.

"YEAH!" Beast let out a roar.

He and Angel ran down the stairs and out of the dorm.

"Yo—wait!" I cried. Too late. The Dum Diddys all ran after them, screaming and waving their wooden swords.

I had no choice. I had to follow them. I shoved the big wad of fives into my pants pocket and took off.

Out on the grass, I could see where Beast and Angel were heading—right to Sherman Oaks and his Knighty Knight Knights at Nyce House.

What had I *done*?

Chapter 18

"ATTACK! DESTROY! WIN!"

The Rotten House Doo-Wah-Diddy Dragons burst into Nyce House, roaring, chanting, waving their swords.

"Whoa—wait! Pause! PAUSE the game!" I shouted. But I was too late.

Beast raised his sword and started slashing away at the curtains. Angel swung hard and shattered a lamp. Crench stabbed a couch and a chair. Feenman was painting the floor red. (That guy just didn't give up with the red paint!)

"Don't wrinkle your costumes!" I shouted. "No

stains! No stains! I have to return them!"

There was no way they could hear me over their screams of attack.

CLANG! CLANG!

Chipmunk and Nosebleed had their helmet-visors down and were head-butting each other. Paintings crashed to the floor.

"ATTACK! ATTACK!"

Belzer screamed. And he stabbed himself in the foot!

It was out of control. I offered one hundred bubus to anyone who would put down his sword and stop fighting. But helmets clanged, and swords slashed and hacked.

And we burst in on Sherman Oaks, Wes Updood, and a bunch of Nyce House dudes in their Commons Room. They didn't hear us coming. They were perched in front of a widescreen TV, clicking away, playing Wungo Warriors.

"SURRENDER, OR ELSE!"

Angel shrieked. The Dum Diddys leaped into the room.

Sherman, the great Wungo Wango, jumped to his feet. His eyes bulged. "Hey—what's up with *this?*" he shouted.

I had to stop it before it got ugly. Or before my costumes ripped.

I grabbed Belzer's sword and ran to the middle of the room. "I claim this dorm in the name of Prince Awesome Dude of the Doo-Wah-Diddy Dum Dibbly Dabbly Doo-dah Dragons!" I shouted. "The Knighty Knight Knights are defeated!"

"Not fair!" Sherman screamed. "Not fair! You can't do this! You don't have access codes from the Wungo Wango. You can't come in here without access codes!"

"We don't need access codes!" Chipmunk shouted. "We've got SWORDS!"

"Not fair!" Sherman wailed. "Not fair!"

Beast swung his sword and hacked the arm off a couch. Angel lowered his helmet-visor and ran headfirst into the TV screen.

"Wait! Stop! Pause the game!" I shouted.

"Sherman is right. It's gotta be a fair battle. I've got plenty of costumes for you guys, too—if you've got the cash!"

I spun Belzer around by the visor. "Belzer, quick—go bring the trunk. We all want a fair battle, right? Get your money out, dudes. Five dollars a costume! Belzer, hurry. We don't want the swords to get cold!"

Belzer took off back to our dorm.

Crench stepped up to me, shaking his head. "Bernie, what are you *doing*? You're gonna rent costumes to the *enemy*?"

I winked at him. "Do you have to ask?"

"But, Bernie—"

"My middle name is *Fairness*," I said. "You know me. I only care about *fairness*. Get your money out, dudes. Five dollars. Come on. No wrinkled bills. I don't have time to iron 'em!"

A few minutes later Belzer returned, groaning, sweating, and lugging the heavy trunk. I heaved the lid open and started handing out capes, helmets, shields, swords, and daggers.

The Nyce House Knighty Knight Knights

grabbed everything I had left. My pockets were bulging with cash.

I slammed the trunk lid shut. It was a signal for the battle to begin.

"It's Dum Dum Doomsday for all Dum Diddys!" Sherman cried. He and his pals charged, screaming and waving their swords.

My Rotten House buddies fought back. Wooden swords clacked. Helmets clanged. Rubber daggers daggered. Belzer stabbed himself in the *other* foot!

Thanks to Bernie B., the Wungo Warriors game came to life. The two sides battled out the front door and onto the grass. The dudes were having an *awesome* time.

It was like a party! Especially for me. I unrolled the wadded-up fives and started to count. "Looks like Prince Awesome Dude is the big winner tonight!" I exclaimed.

But then I looked up from my huge pile of cash. I gasped—and let out a scream of horror.

"NOOOO! NOOOOOOO!"

Chapter 19

"This School Must Be Closed—Tonight!"

Why did I scream?

Because I saw where the battle was heading. To Pooper's Pond!

"Get away!" I went chasing after them, shouting. "Get away from the pond!"

You can barely call it a pond. It's more like a scummy, smelly, muddy ditch. If they fought in Pooper's Pond, the costumes would be caked in its putrid mud.

And who was responsible for the costumes? Bernie B.! I'd have to pay big-time to have them cleaned.

"Get away! Get AWAY!"

Too late.

Beast took a running jump into the pond. Angel followed him in—and everyone else followed Angel.

Swords clacked. Kids screamed and roared. The mud flew.

They rolled in the mud and came up fighting. Knighty Knight Knights and Dum Diddys dove into the muck. Thick gobs of mud oozed down their faces, their capes, their armor.

In seconds, the great battle turned into a disgusting mud bath.

"Not good," I muttered. "Not good at all."

I started to figure what this would cost me. I didn't realize that the horror was just beginning.

Then I turned—and started to choke.

Headmaster Upchuck stood behind me, his eyes goggling out of his head as he stared at the mud fight. Next to him stood five horrified people in gray suits.

The inspectors!

Upchuck pointed a trembling finger at me. "Bernie—I know you're responsible for this!" he cried.

"I—I—I—" It never happened to me before. I was *speechless*!

The shocked inspectors all started talking at once:

"This is an *outrage*!"

"Unspeakable!"

"The students are out of control!"

"They're berserk! Totally berserk!"

"This school must be CLOSED—*tonight*!"

Chapter 20

THE UGLY DUCKLING

"I—I—I—" My brain was still frozen.

And then Mrs. Twinkler stepped forward. She was the only person who didn't look horrified and shocked. She had a big smile on her face.

She strode right up to the inspectors. "This is our annual school pageant!" she told them. "Didn't Bernie do a *fabulous* job?"

"P-pageant?" one inspector stammered. "This ugly mud fight? What kind of pageant is *this*?"

"It's the Battle of Rotten Town of 1650," Mrs. Twinkler told him. She turned to Headmaster

Upchuck. "I *knew* Bernie was the right person to lead the pageant."

Upchuck put a big smile onto his little bald head. "Yes, yes!" he said. "I was the one who picked Bernie. Excellent job, Bernie."

He patted me on the shoulder. "Ha-ha. You inspectors weren't fooled—were you? Did you really think my wonderful students were having a mud fight?"

"It...looked so real," an inspector said. "Wonderful job. I guess."

My brain finally started chugging. "I did my best!" I told them. "But I can't take all the credit. Mrs. Twinkler had the idea to stage it in Pooper's Pond. A *brilliant* idea! I think she deserves a round of applause—don't you?"

The five inspectors clapped.

"The students *all* deserve applause," Mrs. Twinkler said. "Have you ever seen a pageant that looked so *real*?"

"Guess we made a mistake," an inspector said. "I'm very impressed. Best school pageant I ever saw. I think we're all going to file an *excellent* report on this school."

Another inspector squinted at me. "But what is that wad of cash in Bernie's hand?"

I stared down at the money. "Oh, this?" I said. "Just a small gift from my cast and crew. They wanted to show me how much they appreciated all my hard work."

"Bernie is so wonderful," Mrs. Twinkler gushed. "Guess what he's doing. He's giving all that money to the Rotten School Theater Fund." She grabbed the money from my hand.

"This will pay for our second-grade production of *The Ugly Duckling*."

The Ugly Duckling?

My money...my hard-earned money...

Upchuck slapped me on the back. "Congratulations!" he cried. "Job well done!" He and the inspectors turned and walked away.

I watched Mrs. Twinkler counting my money as she trotted off with it.

I let out a long, sad sigh.

"Guess the game is over," Feenman said. I could see only his eyes. He had about three inches of mud all over his face. He looked much better with it.

The other warriors climbed wearily out of the pond. Dudes were dripping mud, groaning and sighing. "I'm toast," Sherman muttered. "Toast."

"I could sleep for a week," Billy the Brain said, yawning.

"Everything HURTS," Beast declared wearily. He started licking mud off his arm.

"What a battle. Thank goodness it's over. We're all totally wrecked." Joe Sweety groaned.

"War is tough," I said. "But remember, dudes—

we're all winners here! Thanks to us, our school is saved!"

Groaning, aching, sighing, we started limping toward our dorms. But we all stopped when we heard the loud, shrill cry.

"WAAAAAA~HOOOOOOOOOOOO!"

I saw Jennifer Ecch first. And then the rest of the girls. In capes and full armor! Waving shiny swords and battle-axes in front of them.

"Prepare to surrender!" Jennifer screamed. "Prepare to surrender to the Dum Dum Daughters of the Doo-Wah-Diddy Dum Dum Diddy Princess!"

"No! Please! Please! Give us a break!"

"We surrender! We surrender!"

"You win!"

The boys' cries couldn't stop the battle. Act Two of the pageant was about to begin! And it was going to be a *slaughter*.

"Belzer, quick!" I said, pulling him aside. "Go get the Nutty Nutty Bars."

He squinted at me. "Bernie, you're still trying to cash in? You're gonna sell candy bars during the battle?"

"No way," I said. "I need something to eat while I watch you fight!"

HERE'S A SNEAK PEEK AT BOOK #13

R.L. STINE'S

ROTTEN SCHOOL

GOT CAKE?

Lighting Up the Dimples

I hurried down the empty hall and stopped at a door at the end. I read the words on the window: ROTTEN EGG.

That's the name of our school yearbook. The *Rotten Egg*. How did it get that name? Who knows? Maybe they just couldn't think of a better one.

I pushed open the door and looked around for the editor. He's a tall, skinny, redheaded sixth grader named Leif Blower.

Blower is really into the yearbook. He has a tiny silver egg stuck through one earlobe. And he wears a green-and-yellow cap that says: ASK ME ABOUT ROTTEN EGGS.

"Yo, Blower! What's up?" I knew he had to be there. He never went to class. He just stayed in the *Rotten Egg* office all day and worked on the yearbook.

Blower had his face buried in a stack of photos on the table in front of him.

He kept shaking his head. "I can't decide," he said. "Bernie, maybe you can help me."

I hurried across the room. "What's the problem?"

He held up three photos. I squinted at them. I saw a window with gray curtains.

"Which photo of Headmaster Upchuck do you like best?" Blower asked.

I squinted at them again. "I don't see Headmaster Upchuck," I said. "I just see a window."

He frowned. "That's the problem. Upchuck is too short. His head didn't come up to the camera lens. I only got the window behind his desk."

"Maybe you should have lowered the camera a little," I said.

Blower scratched his red hair. "Maybe."

I took the photos from his hands and set them

down on the table. "Can we talk?" I said. "I know you've been thinking about my yearbook photo. I'm here to help. I'd like a blue sky in the background. With just a few puffy clouds. Think you can handle that?"

Blower didn't answer. He stared blankly at me.

"I need backlighting," I said. "You know. To capture the silky glow of my hair. I'm not sure which is my best side. You'll have to shoot me from both sides. Then we can decide later—okay?"

He stared at me blankly.

"Or maybe we should do a straight face shot," I said. "I mean, we need to show off *both* of my dimples. Everyone says I have *killer* dimples. Shall we work out special lighting for that? Perhaps a light for each dimple?"

He blinked several times. "Sorry, Bernie," he said. "I didn't hear a word you said."

"But my photo—" I started.

He put a hand on my shoulder. "I've got something much more important to think about, Bernie."

More important than my yearbook picture?

What could that *be*?

"ACK. ACK. ACK."

Blower picked up a bottle from the table and took a long drink from it. He made a face. "This root beer tastes funny."

"It isn't root beer," I told him. I took the bottle and read the label. "India Black Ink."

"ACK. ACK. ACK." Blower grabbed his throat and started hacking and coughing and sputtering.

"You should probably see the nurse," I said. "You're gonna scare people with that black tongue."

"ACK. ACK. ACK."

I picked up the root beer bottle—next to the

bottle of ink—and took a slurp. "But before you go," I said, "can we talk about my photo?"

"ACK. ACK. ACK."

He "acked" for another five or six minutes. Then he did some very loud spitting into a wastebasket.

Finally he sat down. "I think I'm back to normal," he said. His lips were black, and so were his teeth.

"Lookin' good," I said.

Why worry the poor guy?

"About my yearbook photo..." I started.

"Not now," Blower said, shaking his head. "I'm totally thinking about one thing. The Most Popular Rotten Egg."

I stared at him. "The *what?*"

"The yearbook is a hundred years old," he said. "Back then they had the Most Popular Rotten Egg page. They picked the most popular Rotten Student of the year, and the student was named Most Popular Rotten Egg. The student got a whole page in the yearbook all to himself. For the yearbook's hundredth birthday, we're bringing back the tradition."

"Wow! That's excellent!" I cried. I slapped Blower on the back. "This is so sudden. I didn't even know you were thinking of me. But I gladly accept. Shall we take the picture now?"

He stuck out his tongue. "Is my tongue black?"

"Maybe a little," I said. "I'm so excited about the Rotten Egg award."

"Bernie, I haven't decided who wins it," Blower said. "It's a very big responsibility. I'm taking it seriously."

"You won't be sorry," I said. "I'm too modest to say it, but everyone knows that Bernie B. is the most popular dude around here."

"I have to take my time and think hard about it," Blower said. "And I have to discuss it with Mr. Pupipantz, the yearbook adviser."

"I can pose tomorrow afternoon," I told him. "Let me get a haircut first. That'll give you time to talk it over."

Blower scratched his hair. "I'm not so sure you're the winner, Bernie. After all, Sherman Oaks just gave me this video iPod with two hundred movies. That makes him *very* popular with me!"

I gasped. That spoiled rich kid Sherman Oaks was up to his old tricks....